Cruel
A Collection of Wicked Poetry

Ian D Francis

Ian D Francis

Copyright © 2018 Ian D Francis
All rights reserved.
ISBN: 9781731583680
ISBN-13:

Cruella

DEDICATION

I dedicate this book to my family and my true friends, the people who I have loved, and I have laughed with along the way, you're my inspiration. To all those people, and you know who you are, I say thank you, this book would not have been possible without your love, kindness, encouragement and belief.

I also dedicate this book to all those who have cheated and lied along the way, who are there for the good times only, but show their true colours when things start to fall apart. The type of people to whom you reach out for a helping hand in your hour of need, but instead of a helping hand, they deliver a fist to the face. To all those people, and you know who you are, I say thank you, this book would not have been possible without you, you're my inspiration.

Ian D Francis

CONTENTS

	Acknowledgments	i
1	A Gentle Kiss	9
2	The Man in the Iron Mask	11
3	For Whom Tolls the Bell	12
4	Two Little Boys	14
5	A Woman Weeps	16
6	Hitler's Mother	18
7	I Didn't Mean to Kill You	21
8	Poem for the Unknown	22
9	Why?	24
10	A World Gone Mad	25
11	The Poet, the Prostitute and the Priest	26
12	Greed	30
13	Alone and Hungry	32
14	The Kindly Stranger	33
15	Waiting for the Dark	36
16	Foot Soldiers	37
17	Move Over Fatty	39
18	Life in One Day	42
19	Beautiful Butterfly	43
20	This Night	45
21	Gifts	46
22	Weather Forecast	48
23	The Horrible House	49
24	If You Go Down to the Woods Today	52
25	Human Disease	53
26	Painted Lies	54
27	Nothing	56
28	Life is Such	57
29	I'll Meet You in Your Dreams	59
30	Spit in My Eye	60

31	What's My Name?	62
32	The Sorry Beast	64
33	Idle Hands	66
34	The Mobility Scooter Gang of Sunny Benidorm	73
35	Angels Eyes	75
36	Circles	77
37	Bullshit Bingo	78
38	Dead Tired	80
39	She's My Bitch	81
40	The Last Resort	83
41	Drowning in the Same Deep Water as You	86
42	The Sword is Mightier than the Pen	88
43	After the Battle	90
44	Squeak Piggy Squeak	91
45	Mother Waits	93
46	Prince Charmless	94
47	The Day After Redundancy	95
48	Life or Death	96
49	Blood is Thicker than Oil	97
50	When Dinosaurs Ruled the Earth	98

Hidden Bonus Track

About the Author

Other Titles by the Same Author

Ian D Francis

Cruella

ACKNOWLEDGEMENTS

Thank you to
Linda, Heidi, Carly, Lauren, Joshua, Mr Richmond, Lionel,
Stormagen, Finnegan (deceased), Messi, Ronaldo, Harry, Slip, Slop
and all their children and The Poets fans everywhere

Ian D Francis

A GENTLE KISS

This is the last thing that he ever wrote
Simply entitled, 'My Suicide Note'
Took a three-legged bar stool and six feet of rope
And hung himself from his skinny white throat

He could have stayed but it wasn't his style
He swung, and he swayed as he struggled a while
Looked up at the ceiling tiles
The lump in his throat was just vomit and bile

He could hear the tune from that old TV show
But what were the words, yeah how did it go?
Cos suicide is painless which makes it appealing
But things are very different when you're swinging from the ceiling

Then the woman he called
Judy my dear
So much love
So sincere
So much heartache
So many fears
So much suffering
So many years
So many regrets
So many tears
So lucky that day
That she did appear

The key in the lock the door opens wide
A state of shock as she steps inside
Well Johnny rocked, and Johnny writhed
So she grabbed a knife from the kitchen side

Cruella

And there on the fridge stuck with glue
Was the suicide note from Johnny to Jude
She tore it off and read it through
And stood there wondering what to do

Well what to do well what to do
She stood there wondering what she should do
Well Johnny gasped, and his lips turned blue
And then she knew yeah then she knew

She stuck the note back on the fridge
And grabbed old Johnny by the hips
And gently kissed him on his cold blue lips
And softly whispered enjoy your trip

She walked across the kitchen floor
And put the knife back in the drawer
And when Johnny rocked and writhed no more
She went outside and closed the door

The police called in a week or so
The coroner came the case was closed
And there on the fridge a suicide note
The very last thing that he ever wrote

And the morale of the story is simply this
There's nothing more deadly than a gentle kiss

Ian D Francis

MAN IN THE IRON MASK

Hold the smile a fraction too long
And focus on the task
But all alone the smile is gone
The man in the iron mask

I'm fine he says, how are you
Should anybody ask
But inside his heart is broken and torn
The man in the iron mask

The windows of his soul grow dim
The light is fading fast
And no one seems to notice him
The man in the iron mask

And then one day he wasn't there
A figment of the past
Does anybody really care
About the man in the iron mask

FOR WHOM TOLLS THE BELL

You were dragged here from hell
You'll leave in a box
The Lucky Star Motel
Is all out of luck
The cards have been dealt
So basically you're fucked
For you tolls the bell
Your numbers come up

You abandoned your kids
You cheated on your wife
You gambled your savings
And pissed away your life
You live every day
On the edge of a knife
For you tolls the bell
Your numbers come up

So come spin the wheel
Play Russian roulette
Shuffle the pack
And come place your bets
Then it's go Johnny go
On your marks get set
Because for all you know
Your numbers come up

Ian D Francis

You cover your ears
When the baby screams
Then drift away
In a crack pipe dream
Your life is falling
Apart at the seams
Stick twist or bust
Your numbers come up

You never count your losses
Because the fun never ends
There's some fat balding tossers
You once called your friends
If you could turn back the clock
You'd change everything
For you tolls the bell
Your numbers come up

There is no happy ending
To this tale that I tell
You live out your days
In a cold empty cell
And the hangman is waiting
To send you to hell
Your numbers come up
For you tolls the bell

Cruella

TWO LITTLE BOYS

Two little boys had two little toys
Each had a nuclear warhead
Gaily they'd say, bombs away
And a million people lay dead

Tony has got some soldiers
And George has got some tanks
It's the perfect foil now they've got the oil
You can tell the UN no thanks

We are fighting a war on terror
But we've lost their hearts and minds
Democracy the American dream
Is on trial for its war crimes

We talk about collateral damage
When an innocent civilian dies
Aint life a bitch the corrupt get rich
It was all a bunch of lies

Tony and George are laughing
Now the missiles have been deployed
And I wonder if the World will remember
When they were two little boys

Meanwhile the cities are burning
And insurgence rule the streets
It's total chaos but we don't give a toss
There never were any WMDs

Ian D Francis

All the people are living in fear
On the brink of a civil war
But we don't give a damn remember Vietnam
We have been here once before

We are whipping up a Desert Storm
All across the Middle East
It's an evil little plot but there's something we forgot
Because we haven't got an exit strategy

Has anyone seen Osama
Because we don't know where he's gone
But the biggest terrorist is missing from the list
And is hiding in Washington

Tony and George are laughing
Now the World has been destroyed
And I wonder if the World will remember
When they were two little boys

And I wonder if the World will remember
When they were two little boys

Cruella

A WOMAN WEEPS

Inner anger
Outward fury
You are the judged
He is the jury
Storm
Frenzy
Hatred
Violence
Sssshhhhh!
Deadly silence

An accusation
A violent rage
Push the eject
And get away
Passion
Mania
Adrenalin rush
Sssshhhhh!
A deadly hush

Try malfeasance
Misfortune rejoices
Try malengine
And threatening voices
Intimidation
Hostility
Malice
Ill will
Sssshhhhh!
And lie still

Ian D Francis

It's either or
Him that chooses
So cover your face
And hide the bruises
Inhumanity
Insanity
The devil sleeps
Sssshhhhh!
A woman weeps

Cruella

HITLER'S MOTHER

A Mother's curse
Mothers kiss
Mother calls
Mothers' milk

Mother church
Mother of thyme
Mother country
Mother of mine

Mother city
Mother craft
Mother nature
Mother's mark

Fits of Mother
Mothers' wit
Mother liquor
Mothership

Mother naked
Her Mother's daughter
Mothering Sunday
Mother water

Mother of souls
Motherhood
Every Mother's son
Mother of all good

Mother of millions
Mother of pearl
Mother's boy
Mother's girl

Mother water
Motherwort
Mother tongue
A Mother's retort

Mother hen
Motherless
Mother in law
Mother knows best

Old Mother Hubbard
Motherly
Mothers' meeting
Mother me

Mother Carey's chicken
A Mother's doing
Watch with Mother
Mothers ruin

Motherly love
Mother of Christ
A Mothers tears
A Mothers price

Mothers' pride
Mothers' hand
Mother of all battles
In the Motherland

Cruella

Mother of death
Mother of birth
Mother fist
Mother earth

Mother of all evil
Mother of doom
A Mother fucker
In a Mother's womb

I DIDN'T MEAN TO KILL YOU

I didn't mean to kill you
Well perhaps just a little
I didn't know you'd snap
Didn't think you'd be so brittle
In a moments heightened pleasure
I wasn't aware of any complaints
With the writhing of your body
And the pulling on your restraints
As your eyes rolled in their sockets
My thoughts were not of murder
But amidst the rattling of the bedposts
I guess I never heard you
Then as I gently squeezed your throat
A momentary lapse
But I didn't mean to kill you
But then again……..
Perhaps

Cruella

POEM FOR THE UNKNOWN

A dealer deals in the underpass
The decks been shuffled
But the cards are marked
A junkie knows this could be his last
But the cravings are coming
And they're coming fast

Alone on a bridge a young girl cries
Looking for one thing good in her life
She's had too much of her daddy's abuse
So she buys a rope then ties a noose
A short sharp crack as the traffic flies by
Just another teenage suicide

A siren wails in a high-speed chase
It's winner takes all in a two-car race
A serial thief out for a ride
Hits a young woman with a baby inside
Fights for her life in a sea of red
Then a stranger whispers 'Your baby's dead'

A fight breaks out at closing time
The odds are stacked it's one against nine
Through the dark streets a frantic chase
The wolves smell blood there's no escape
Drops to his knees as the pack close in
His only crime the colour of his skin

Ian D Francis

A young woman searches in an empty purse
Locked in a marriage for better or worse
He's out drinking chatting up whores
Smoking drugs or something worse
Two black eyes for her bad behaviour
The only thing he ever gave her

A homeless man down on his luck
Searches in the gutter for a cigarette butt
Wanders off in the chill of the night
To make his bed beneath a street light
Dreams of his wife how he longs for her kiss
A minute with her than a lifetime of this
For a few precious moments they're together again
Wakes from his dream when it starts to rain

In a crowded club the members stand
Love and hate tattoos on the knuckles of their hands
A thousand-yard stare says come and try it
One false move can start a riot
A midnight meet by the council flats
They've got no balls, but they bought some bats

A young man lies in the pouring rain
A dirty needle in his vein
The wilted flowers in a plastic vase
Where a junkie died in the underpass

Cruella

WHY?

Her daddy left home
 and the little girl cried

Her mama got sick
 and was too weak to fight

She wrote to her lover
 but he never replied

She fell to her knees
 and she asked the lord why?

Why did my daddy
 leave me all alone?

Why is my mama
 just skin and bone?

Why does my lover
 never come home?

And why-why lord
 won't you pick up the phone?

Ian D Francis

A WORLD GONE MAD

When he completed his journey from riches to rags
He packed up his life in two Safeway bags
The repo co had taken his car
So he wandered down to his local bar
Drowned his sorrows one last time
Then went to the phone and dialed 999
The police they sent just a slip of a girl
Who heard him mutter 'Goodbye cruel World'
Put a magnum between his gums
And blew himself to kingdom come

Next door at the W.I.
An OAP prays help me die
Cos whatever I do it's never enough
It's a hard-old life and I'm just not tough
Plucks up courage through pills and drink
Then dives head long from the bathroom sink
Smashes her skull on the porcelain
They just swept the pieces down the drain

The Kyoto treaty remains unsigned
The icecaps melt and the seas they rise
G8 leaders ignore the warnings
Of El Nino and of global warming
Send African children to the slaughter
Whilst New Orleans lies under water
Meanwhile in the Pacific Ocean
A nuclear test is set in motion
It's kind of funny and it's kind of sad
Just another example of a World gone mad

Cruella

THE POET, THE PROSTITUTE AND THE PRIEST

She's the centre-fold
In a magazine
Every young man's
Fantasy
The billboard poster
Looking down on the street
The forbidden fruit
Of a catholic priest

The congregation
Titter tatter
The poet has
His subject matter
Homeless
Penniless
Destitute
Forced to be
A prostitute
Feed the hungry
Feed the lean
Feed the pimps
Feed the machine
Girls of all ages
Take your pick
Tightly grasp
Your crucifix
The devil whispers
Take a fix
Dial 0800
666

All girl action
On the silver screen
Internet porn
In a silicone dream
A triple X rated
Frustrated
Cum-junkie
Sits alone
And spanks the monkey
Spread yourself
Let me feast
The forbidden fruit
Of a catholic priest

Calling cards
In a telephone box
Explicit poses
Designed to shock
Come Armageddon
Come the revolution
Come free my body
From prostitution
The collection plate
The congregation
Give generously
To the restoration
Buy a place in heaven
Buy salvation
Ignore the homeless
At the railway station
Homeless
Penniless
Destitute
And the poet writes
About a prostitute

Cruella

Those most in need
We help the least
The forbidden fruit
Of the catholic priest

Here's the church
Here's the steeple
No one cares
About desperate people
Cleanse my soul
Grant absolution
And deliver me
From prostitution
Fetishes
Fantasies
Sadistic urges
Judges
Barristers
And the clergy
Renounce your sins
In confessional
And fuck the needy
Fuck them all

Teenage lust
Man's wet dream
Never enough
Until you hear her scream
Treat her rough
She's only fourteen
A crying
Weeping
Effigy
Of the innocent child
She used to be

Take her body
Pray to Christ
And deliver me
From a life of vice
Name your pleasure
Name your price
And when you look to heaven
Do you see a red light?

So, come….
All ye unfaithful
Come and see
It's the unholy disorder
Of blasphemy
Where everyone's
An atheist
The poet
The prostitute
And the priest

She's the centre-fold
In a magazine
Every young man's
Fantasy
Pouting
Panting
Between the sheets
The forbidden fruit
Of a catholic priest
Homeless
Penniless
Destitute
And the poet writes
About a prostitute
Renounce your sins

Cruella

In confessional
And fuck the needy
Fuck them all

Ian D Francis

GREED

Hide said the serpent
Hide said the fox
Hide said the jack
As he climbed in his box

Fly said the eagle
Fly said the jay
Fly dragon fly
Fly fly away

No said the leopard
As he padded through the snow
No said the bear
No no no!

Run said the lion
Run said the deer
Run said the tiger
Run far from here

No said the rhino
No said the ape
No said the tortoise
No time to escape

Soon said the elephant
Soon said the lynx
Soon said the albatross
We'll all be extinct

Cruella

Climb said the gibbon
Climb the chimpanzee
Climb said the python
High in the tree

Dive said the dolphin
The whale and hammerhead
Dive to the deep
Lay on the bed

Mine said the greedy pig
With his snout in the trough
Mine said the greedy swine
I'll never have enough

Mine said the greedy pig
All mine said the swine
Took his fill from the swill
And snorted mine all mine

Ian D Francis

ALONE AND HUNGRY

Lonely is the night
Without the stars above
Lonely is the bride
Who never tasted love
Lonely is the desert
Drier than a stone
And lonely is the bitter wind
That chills her to the bone

Hungry is the mother
Without a grain of corn
Hungry will the child be
If it's ever born
Hungry is the nagging pain
That will not be ignored
And hungry is the wolf
That's waiting at her door

Cruella

THE KINDLY STRANGER

Everybody ran
From the scene of the crime
Fingerprints were found
But none of them were mine
The police they got their man
And now he's doing time

Drama did unfold
When the case was tried
The evidence was lost
The star witness lied
The jury was unanimous
No leniency applied

He rotted in his cell
No one to call a friend
No letters did arrive
No letters did he send
No happy ever after
No this is not the end

His father sat and drank
His mother sat and cried
His brother robbed a bank
Then committed suicide
And who should they all thank
Well I'll let you decide

Ian D Francis

Now do I feel remorse
And do I feel ashamed
The answer is of course
Because I put him in the frame
But I tell you this my friend
I would do it all again

The world passed slowly by
At the pleasure of The Queen
They gave him twenty years
But he was out in seventeen
Broken and confused
With nothing in between

He drifted for a while
He moved from town to town
He couldn't get a job
So he couldn't settle down
Was last seen on a bridge
Presumably he drowned

And what became of me
Well I am doing fine
I met a kindly stranger
As I ran from the crime
I think about him now and then
From time to time to time

And in moments such as these
Fortunes are lost and made
As we play out the scenes
From life's little charade
Our private thoughts exposed
Our privates on parade

Cruella

The sun slowly sets
The light slowly fades
The policeman quickly ran
The sirens quickly wailed
And so the snare was set
And so the trap was laid

A world turned upside down
From far beyond the pale
A kindly stranger passing by
A stranger to my aid
Liberty a heavy price
His prints upon the blade

Ian D Francis

WAITING FOR THE DARK

It took her far too long to realise
Then like a hammer it hit her between the eyes
That most of what he said was lies
And the rest?
Well that was simply not true

She gave to him her youthful years
And all she has to show is a million tears
Which she keeps in buckets underneath the stairs
But the saddest thing of all
Is that no one really cares

Well nature took her babies
And life it broke her heart
Now she hums a lullaby
As she's waiting in the dark
Well nature took her babies
And life it broke her heart
Now she listens for a cry
As she waits in the dark

Stop looking for a reason
There's nothing to be said
This is the screaming season
But only in her head
Stop looking for a Jesus
A shroud to wrap your head
And the screaming gets so loud
It's enough to wake the dead
Enough to wake the dead

Cruella

FOOT SOLDIERS

Goose stepping
March in time
Two by two
And nein by nein
They hide in shadows
So you cannot see
The foot soldiers
Of the BNP

Speak in whispers
Leave no trace
They come and go
This master race
In house and home
And factory
The foot soldiers
Of the BNP

Radicalized
The infection spreads
Swastikas
And double ZZs
The Fatherland
In parody
The foot soldiers
Of the BNP

Ian D Francis

The Holocaust
They do deny
Repatriation
Au revoir goodbye
The U-Boats
Far out at sea
The foot soldiers
Of the BNP

Nazi salutes
And shaven heads
Jack boots
And brain deads
Nick Griffin
Spread your disease
The foot soldiers
Of the BNP

Cruella

MOVE OVER FATTY

I'm walking through the high street
I'm looking for a place to eat
But every high street looks the same
The same old chains it's such a shame
And I can't find a thing I want
Just a bunch of fast food restaurants
But I walk into one just the same
So maybe I'm to blame

There's a finger-licking chicken place
Where you can go to stuff your face
Blocked arteries are guaranteed
To help you leave the human race
Where the burger meals are happy
Because they come with plastic crappy toys
And a nation full of girls and boys
Are heading for obesity
Well that don't sound so good to me
No that don't sound so happy
So you can take your plastic crappy toys
And shove them up your jacksy

I'm looking for a place to sit
There's just one space and this is it
And the bloke who's sitting next to me
Is big and round and sweaty
They say that gluttony is a sin
There's ketchup on his treble chin
So I ask him all politely
Move over fatty

Ian D Francis

Yeah move over fatty
Let's start a revolution
It may not be PC
But it could be a solution
And if you've got a better one
Then baby I'm all ears
I'm gonna sing this little song
So that everybody hears

So we eat our food and don't say nothing
As he tucks into an Egg McMuffin
With ribs and dips and chips and thighs
Hey fatty, who ate all the pies?
And half the World is hungry
While the other half has plenty
We see pictures on our tellies
As we supersize our bellies

I wish we'd all take what we need
And feed the children of the World
Take a little exercise
And consume a little less
Then maybe we'd be happy
And maybe we'd be healthy
And stop blaming immigration
For the problems of the NHS

So move over fatty
There's no need to be so greedy
There's got to be a way to help
The hungry and the needy
If there's a government strategy
Well I aint heard it yet
But we could start by scrapping Trident
And wipe out third world debt

Cruella

But the country voted Brexit
And nothing now can stop
Race hate crime is on the rise
The Poles are being polarized
The burkini ban an Brighton beach
And soon their gonna ban free speech
So rise up now while we are free
And sing this little song with me

So move over fatty
Let's start a revolution
It may not be PC
But it could be a solution
And if you've got a better one
Then baby I'm all ears
I'm gonna sing this little song
So that everybody hears

The earth so full of riches
Is controlled by sons of bitches
They're filling up their pockets
As they test their nuclear rockets
So everybody run and hide
They're plotting global genocide
So put your head between your legs
And kiss your arse goodbye

Ian D Francis

LIFE IN ONE DAY

Born at the stroke of dawn
Into a heartless world
Her mother left her on a bench
A nameless little girl
She met him in the morning
Fell in love by afternoon
They married in the evening
Then went on honeymoon
Fell pregnant in the midnight hour
By breakfast he had fled
Suffered from a broken heart
By lunch time she was dead
They took her to a cemetery
On the far side of town
And there they laid her bones to rest
As the sun was going down
The preacher stood all alone
Not a single mourner came
With nothing carved upon the stone
For no one knew her name

BEAUTIFUL BUTTERFLY

I sat upon the clifftop
Looking out to sea
The waves crashed against the rocks
And sprayed a cooling scree
Then delicate and gentle
Floating on the breeze
A beautiful butterfly
Came to rest on me
I remembered what she said to me
I remembered what she said to me

Underneath a giant oak
The rare beauty on my knee
I dare not move a muscle because
The butterfly would flee
And sitting in the whispering grass
A rabbit young and shy
Dined upon the meadow flowers
Beneath a sun kissed sky
Contented in the summertime
One, two, three
I remembered what she said to me
I remembered what she said to me

Dancing in the treetops
High above our heads
Feasting on the acorns
His tail of crimson red
The ocean kissed the shoreline
Caressed the golden sand
In a parallel universe
We're walking hand-in-hand
I am holding yours

But you are holding his
It was only a kiss
It was only a kiss
I remembered what she said to me
It was only a kiss

Gathering in the distance
Clouds so dark and grey
Descend upon the big oak tree
And chase the red away
The oil slickened ocean
Sticking to the rocks
The lifeless bloodied rabbit
In the jaws of a fox
I remembered what she said to me
It was only a kiss
The beautiful butterfly
Crushed within my fist
It was only a kiss
It was only a kiss
I remembered what she said to me
It was only a kiss

Cruella

THIS NIGHT

All alone in an empty bed
I turned to you and softly said
Can I hold you through this winter's night?
And when your answer never came
I bundled up this house of pain
In the cold damp sheets of an empty bed
I'll never sleep again

Feeling low and fading fast
I turned to you and politely asked
May I lay my weary head upon your breast
Each night your answer is the same
Stony silence, driving rain
In the cold damp sheets of an empty bed
I'll never sleep again

GIFTS

These are my lips
Yours to kiss
These are my charms
Can you resist?
This is my hand
Yours to hold
This is my story
Or so it is told
This is my promise
Never to break
This is the love
I want you to take
These are my dreams
Keep them with yours
These are my words
These are my thoughts
These my possessions
My castle and keep
These are my arms
To rock you to sleep
This is my heart
Yours to beat
These are the gifts
I give them to thee

Cruella

These are the buckets
Of tears I have wept
This is your secret
The one that you kept
This is your lover
He is not me
Forsaken for another
How can that be?
This is the time
You spent on your back
This is the thrill
You had in the sack
This is your truth
Brutal and cold
This is your love
Easily sold
Here's the deceit
And the lies you have told
Yours is the beauty
I'll never behold
This is our love
Cloaked all in black
The gifts that I gave
I take them all back

Ian D Francis

WEATHER FORECAST

The good Lord sent the cleansing rain
To wash away their sins
The Devil sent a lightning bolt
To expose them all again
The good Lord sent the thunder
To sound a mighty warning
The Devil scorched the bone-dry earth
And called it global warming
The Almighty gathered up the folk
And told them all to pray
The Devil summoned up the wind
And blew them all away

Cruella

THE HORRIBLE HOUSE

The orphan house
Is a horrible house
Where nobody speaks
And everyone shouts
At night we sneak
As quiet as a mouse
While the beasties sleep
In the horrible house

In the dead of night
When all is still
By silver light
We climb the hill
Past the place
Where the church once stood
Across the field
And through the wood
We jump the stream
Then double back
To the horrible house
At the end of the track

Late at night
When darkness stirs
No one knows
What might occur
Something moves
With cloven hooves
Piercing eyes
And knotted fur

Ian D Francis

The children cower
In their beds
And pull the sheets
Above their heads
While a witch's bitch
Without a stitch
Dances with the dead
They dance until the sunrise
Serenade until the dawn
Ghosts and ghouls
And ignorant fools
All Satan's deadly spawn
Morning brings the madness
An unprovoked attack
But everybody looks away
In the horrible house
At the end of the track

Everybody's hungry
But no one says a word
Her policies are unfair, but firm
Children should be seen, but
Children should not be heard

The beasts of prey
Sleep by day
And to ensure the rules
Are all obeyed
The toys are packed away
There'll be no play today
So they all sit in silence
And await the violence
To start all over again
In this unhappy house of pain
Where humanity lacks

Cruella

In the horrible house
At the end of the track

Then...
One day
While to beasties slept
One boy crept
Into the kitchen
Where the matches were kept
Then fastened all the latches
Of the doors
From the outside

Then the orphan girls
And the orphan boys
Gathered up the forbidden toys
And piled them all together
And built themselves a pyre
Then lit themselves a fire
Soon the flames grew wild
And the flames grew higher
And higher
Until the house was all ablaze
Then they ran outside
Into the day
And the beasties cries
Filled the skies
As the timbers cracked
In the sinister shack
And the sky turned from perfect blue
To perfect black
Then the children smiled
And never went back
To the horrible house
At the end of the track

Ian D Francis

IF YOU GO DOWN TO THE WOODS TODAY

Don't go down to the woods boy
Some things you shouldn't see
You'll find your lover just hanging around
Hanging from a tree
She saw you hanging with that girl
You hung on her every word
Couldn't hang on to your memory
Couldn't hang on to her dreams

So don't go down to the woods today
You're sure to be surprised
Her neck is snapped like a twig
The buzzards peck her eyes
If you go down to the woods today
You're sure to be surprised
The ground is soaked by a lover's tears
As she committed suicide

So don't go down to the woods today
Some things you shouldn't see
No don't go down to the woods today
For hanging there is me

HUMAN DISEASE

Shrapnel flies
Drop to your knees
Look to the sky
Dappled trees
Whisper why
Catch the breeze
Say goodbye
Ask pretty please
A son cries
A mother bleeds
Another dies
A human disease

Ian D Francis

PAINTED LIES

She lies to him through a painted smile
And whispers can I stay a while
She has the looks she has the style
To have any man she wants

This is all there's nothing more
Her still warm dress lays on the floor
As she stands before him naked
As the day that she was born

To be or not to be
That is her question
There is no us there is only me
But tonight, I'll make an exception

He said I recognise those painted lies
I've heard them all before
I have no love to give you
But darling I forgive you
I have no choice this golden voice
Is a curse that I must live with

She said I don't need forgiveness
I'm really not religious
All I need's your poetry
You silver tongued linguist
Yeah we've been here before son
But your poetry is awesome
Give me Yeats and Keats between the sheets
Yeah let's all have a foursome

Cruella

And what lies beneath this lipstick
Are the lips that I shall kiss with
I'll do anything you want me too
No painted lies just painted truths
Forgive me for the crimes of youth
Though I tried my best I failed the test
Won't you place your hand upon my breast

Because I don't need forgiveness
I'm really not religious
Just fuck me hard you handsome bard
Then ravish and deprave me
Jesus cannot save me
Come grab my hips and kiss my lips
For old times' sake yeah baby

So one for the road
For old times' sake maybe
The years have gone by
But the flames still burn bright baby
In the morning we'll be strangers
And this night we will forget
So grab my hips and kiss my lips
For old times' sake yeah baby

Ian D Francis

NOTHING

The devil cast his seed
It landed on your foetus
Now you carry a vile disease
And I don't mean diabetes
Your life is just an empty shell
And you are long since dead
Poison flows through your veins
And there's shit inside your head
Now the doctors gather round your bed
And curse and frown and scratch their heads
Then toss away their gowns and in unison they said
A miracle we cannot perform
Upon the stillborn spawn of the sick and depraved
Take him to his grave
There's nothing left to save
There's nothing left to save
There's nothing left
There's nothing
Nothing at all
(Was there ever?)

Cruella

LIFE IS SUCH

It's unbelievable I know but true
I said to the tramp with the Big Issues
I'm finding life so tough
And I haven't got enough
And how I wish that I had more

He put a bony hand up to his brow
Then scratched his chin and said well listen now
I've a story to tell
About a man I once knew well
Who looked a lot like me

He dropped his eyes down to the gutter
And eventually began to mutter
Let me tell you boy what I have seen
I once thought that the grass was green
On the other side

But there aint no use in wishing for
The things that just aren't there no more
And your screams just get louder
Amidst the needles and the powder
But no one's listening

And upon the opium scented breeze
All the whoring and the sleaze
That funds your vile existence
Means your friends keep their distance
Or cross the road to avoid you

Ian D Francis

In a darkened doorway all alone
A pile of rancid skin and bone
That fortune could not save
A traveller to the grave
Waiting for the reaper

So go ahead and wish away
And you could be like me someday
You have so very much
And maybe life is such
That we are already one

I'LL MEET YOU IN YOUR DREAMS

As you were sleeping lover
Into your room I crept
I climbed into your bed
And held you as you slept
Your body soft and warm
The memory mine to keep
I lay my weary head
And drifted into sleep
I dreamt I cut you open
Then sat and watched you bleed
A crimson tide flowed from your veins
And washed the sin from me
Then I tenderly dressed your wounds
And gently soothed your pain
Then I sliced you up once more
And watched you bleed again
I woke up so invigorated
But you, you did not stir
I turned the pillow
Brushed the sheet
As though I was never there
Closed the door went outside
Into the cold crisp dew
And as I passed your window
My mind reached out to you
As you awoke from troubled sleep
Are things ever as they seem?
Until we meet again my love
I'll meet you in your dreams

Ian D Francis

SPIT IN MY EYE

You can dog-ear my pages
Spill coffee on my leaves
Take me in stages
Just an hour a week
One after the other
All in one day
Pick me up
Put me down
Or just put me away
Dirty my cover
Leave me crumpled and creased
Take me as your lover
Smear me in grease
Visit me once
Or again and again
Leave me out in the sun
The wind and the rain
In the front of your car
Or the back of your mind
Use and abuse me
Treat me gentle and kind
I can make you so angry
I can help you unwind
Get lost forever
Or be easy to find
On the outside shallow
On the inside deep
I can keep you awake
Or rock you to sleep
You can read my thoughts
Get inside my mind
Look for hidden meanings
Between the lines

Cruella

Only a privileged few
Know me well
I'll share my secrets with you
But you must never tell
And if you kissed me goodbye
Would my lipstick be smudged?
You can spit in my eye
But leave me unjudged

Ian D Francis

WHAT'S MY NAME?

I said to my mother
What's my daddies name mama
She said it could be
Or it might be some other
A tall handsome stranger
On the first day of summer
Who never told me his name
But he asked me so politely
If he could spend the night
And when I looked in his eyes so blue
Well what's a girl to do?

What's my name mama
What's my name?
What's my name mama
What's my name?
You hook me
You gut me
You slice me
You cut me
You never even loved me
And you don't know
What's my name?

I said to my woman
Do you still love me honey?
She said it could be
I'm just after your money
A cutting remark
Which I didn't find funny
No I'm not laughing at all
And the baby cries in his manger
And the wolf he howls at the moon

Cruella

And I see in his eyes a stranger
When I look in his eyes so blue

What's my name mama
What's my name?
What's my name mama
What's my name?
You hook me
You gut me
You slice me
You cut me
You never even loved me
And you don't know
What's my name?

Ian D Francis

THE SORRY BEAST

The beast it is sleeping now
Don't wake it from its slumber
It dreams of being an eight
But is a much lower number
Crushed by a lover
Now choosing to refrain
This sorry beast will never rise again

The world so full of wonder
Implodes into abyss
Empty days and lonely nights
Spent longing for her kiss
Devoid of any feelings
Of love or pleasure or pain
This sorry beast will never rise again

So take your filthy hands
From its emaciated neck
Sex is just sex
Without the joy of her caress
The limp lifeless flesh
You look upon with disdain
This sorry beast will never rise again

Never shall desire call
Never shall it feast
Never shall the midday sun
Shine upon this beast
Never shall it ever be
Totally at peace
And never shall it rise again
This sorry little beast

MARCEL BROODTHAERS

These are the poems that will never be read
This is the prose that will never be said
Only discovered long after I'm dead
Yeah these are the poems that will never be read

These are the pages that will never be turned
These are the lessons that nobody learned
Faded from memory like a lover spurned
Yeah these are the pages that nobody turned

These are the thoughts that will never be shared
Lost in time because nobody cares
Entombed in cement like Marcel Broodthaers
Yeah these are the thoughts that will never be shared

These are my footsteps beware you tread
These are the tears that will never be shed
Written in black or colitis red
Yeah these are my footsteps beware you tread

These are the poems that nobody read
Covered in dust under the bed
Up in the attic or down in the shed
Only discovered long after I'm dead

These are the poems that nobody read

Ian D Francis

IDLE HANDS

Gather round people
I've a story to tell
Of how I came to be in prison
Rotting in this cell
And the hangman is waiting
To send me to hell
So gather round people
And my story I will tell

I was born in an ugly little town in the east
The midwife did declare
He's got the eyes of the beast
My mother crossed herself
And grabbed her crucifix
The birthmark on my head
Read number six six six

I wasn't what you'd call
A cute little baby
The nannies never hung around
Longer than a year
They said that I was strange
And they were right to be afraid
Because the ones that didn't leave
Would simply disappear

Cruella

By a cruel twist of fate
When I was nearly eight
They sent me to the asylum
For disturbed little boys
Well the rooms were all padded
And the windows were all barred
But I'd still live there now
If they gave me a choice

On Christmas eve just for kicks
I wrote to Santa with my list
Of all the things I wanted
Him to bring me on his sleigh
An axe and some chain
And various restraints
I cursed that old bastard
When he left me a train

So on the first day of Christmas
I drew up a list
Of all those motherfuckers
And those that I wished
I could strike from the earth
Or simply blow away
And the list grew longer
With every passing day

The devil will find work
Or so the saying goes
For idle hands to plot the end
Of all his hated foes
And on the twelve days of Christmas
They were gonna have to pay
I sent the list to Santa Claus
A different kind of slay

Ian D Francis

Father Robert had it coming
I never liked him much
He preyed upon the altar boys
Cursed by his touch
He offered absolution
Sat upon his knee
And on the first day of Christmas
They found him hanging from a tree

I'm dreaming of a pure white
Christmas don't you know
Powder white crystals
That feed the nations nose
The dealers who deal in misery
That rob the youth of life
Lay naked in the blizzard
Frozen in the ice

On the third day of Christmas
A drunk driver said to me
I killed a mother and her child
Walking down the street
He pulled at the seatbelt
And screamed with remorse
As the car filled with fumes
From a pipe in the exhaust

On day four they found nurse Molly
Up at Parsons Lake
The rocks in her pockets
Helped to seal her fate
The police they can't explain
But suspicion does abound
Why the old folks live much longer
Now nurse Molly's not around

Cruella

On the fifth day of Christmas
A thief and his bling
Stolen from the family home
Five gold rings
The ones your mother gave you
Upon her dying bed
So no one shed a tear
When the thief lay dead

On the sixth day of Christmas
I was feeling kind of wild
I gave a special present
To my parents favourite child
And I laughed and I schemed
As I frolicked with my sister
Until she snapped her pretty neck
In a festive game of Twister

Well my parents were distressed
So my father did suggest
That I move to an address
Far from the scene
And as I was leaving
I vowed to get even
So I returned the next day
With a can of gasoline

Well I seem to remember
As they sifted through the embers
Finding their remains
And feeling such remorse
If I'd have planned it better
I've have burned the Irish setter
Those mangy fucking cats
And the thoroughbred horse

Unsurprisingly by now
Suspicions were aroused
So a copper came around
And I invited him inside
And as he snooped for clues
I slipped his head into a noose
And when I kicked away the chair
He turned a shade of blue

I've lost count of the days
And all the different ways
I have reaped my own kind of vengeance
To those on my list
And my levels of depravity
Defy the laws of gravity
I've grown to like the killing
To this I must confess

Old Mrs. Rosie Raven
Was counting out her savings
She was planning to retire
And live by the coast
As she counted out the bills
She popped too many pills
So the coroner concluded
That she took an overdose

Well I shed a little tear
When the clock struck New Year
At the fireworks display
At the end of the pier
And the truth was never learned
Of how the rockets were all turned
And shot towards the crowds
Who had gathered there to cheer

Cruella

Well panic spread fast
As the rockets flew past
It's every man for himself
In the ensuing stampede
There was screaming and crying
As the people lay dying
For Auld Lang Syne
Here's to a gruesome end

The corpses kept on mounting
The townsfolk were a counting
They said this ugly little town
By the devil must be cursed
That they would never be free
And I tend to agree
So as it went from bad to worse
They locked themselves inside the church

So with the church doors locked
Opportunity knocks
So many townsfolk
In one place at one time
And as darkness closes in
My ultimate sin
Was to replace all the candles
With sticks of dynamite

Praying on their knees
Begging Lord please
All it took was a match
To blow the church to smithereens
And all far too late
When they did investigate
It didn't take a genius
To know it was all because of me

Ian D Francis

Well that's the end of Jackanory
And my gruesome little story
Has come to an end
Or so everybody thinks
But ask yourself this question
As I held your attention
Did you notice that I dropped
A little something in your drinks

As you gasp and you choke
It appears that the joke
Is on the observers who came
To witness my death
So I'll wish you a goodbye
And as you slowly die
I'll be killing and slaying
In an ugly little town in the West

It's a sorry little tale
I'm sure you will agree

Cruella

MOBILITY SCOOTER GANG OF SUNNY BENIDORM

They're tearing up the pavement
They terrorise the streets
They're the Brits abroad you've heard about
But never want to meet
They're ripping up the disco
They're kicking up a storm
The mobility scooter gang
Of sunny Benidorm

With a full English breakfast
Rumbling round inside
They're getting on their scooters
And going for a ride
Down to the English pub
Where the beer is served lukewarm
The crinkly wrinkly dimply gang
Of sunny Benidorm

Fish and chips and Sunday roasts
Happy hour all day
Leather skin and double chins
Soaking up the rays
Beer bellies all on show
Tattoos by the score
The bingo bashing badass gang
Of sunny Benidorm

Ian D Francis

Elvis tribute theme bars
Union Jack shorts
Bikini clad grandmother fuckers
Who've grown too fat to walk
They want to live in England
But England abroad
The sleazy cheesy creasey gang
Of Sunny Benidorm

ANGELS EYES

I hear the angels cry
Heavenly rain falls from way up high
As the Angel Gabriel asks him is it time to die
To be free of pain
To be free of life

I got this cruel disease
It grips and twists and brings me to my knees
I pray to Jesus
Lord help me please

The good lord told us I will come again
Let me take away son, all your pain
You will live in peace for eternity
You'll be seated here right next to me

But I don't want to sleep
There's so many women I have yet to meet
I may be crippled, and I may be weak
I may be disfigured, and I might be a freak
But I aint dying
No not today
So stop your crying
Wipe the tears away
My angel eyes
My angel eyes
This aint goodbye
My angel eyes

Ian D Francis

Survival by any means
Cling to my bible
In a crack pipe dream
Smoke dope to cope
Or use amphetamines

Well Mr. Pharmacist
Open up your store
You know I can't resist
Drift away for a while
And forget about everything

And as I sleep I see how it used to be
Walking hand in hand my baby next to me
We could be on the Strand it could be any street
I aint crippled and I aint weak
I aint disfigured and I aint no freak
And I'm not dying
No not today
So stop your crying
Wipe your tears away
My angel eyes
My angel eyes
This aint goodbye
My angel eyes

CIRCLES

You sleep
You dream
You wake
Hit the alarm
Stretch
Yawn
Get out of bed
Look in the Mirror
Is that really me?
Wash
Dress
Eat
Say goodbye
Drive to work
Say hello
Check your watch
Do your thing
Check your watch
Say goodbye
Drive home
Say hello
Eat
Undress
Wash
Look in the mirror
Is that really me?
Yawn
Stretch
Set the alarm
You sleep
You dream
You wake………

Ian D Francis

BULLSHIT BINGO

Monday bright and early
But I don't want to go
A day of endless meetings
Playing bullshit bingo
We sit around and all talk shite
From early morn to late at night
And hope the economy's alright
Because we don't have a clue

Tuesday at the station
I've got my briefcase in my hand
With a copy of the Metro
And a cheese and pickle sand-
wich I made last night with stale bread
Just before I climbed into my bed
And dreamt that I was anywhere instead
Of bullshit bingo land

Wednesday in the think-tank
Clichés come thick and fast
If everybody's on the bus
Then nail your colours to the mast
There's no I in team dare to dream
It makes me want to scream
The minutes drag so slowly by
It's bullshit bingo time

Cruella

Thursday we get creative
Which roughly translated
Means we sit around in circles
And write on flipchart paper
The team building exercise
Is everything that I despise
So you can take your yellow Post-it notes
And shove them up your seminars

On Friday there's a briefing
It's time for blue sky thinking
As the CEO announces
That the company is shrinking
They call it downsizing
And it's really not surprising
The country is in recession
It's really quite depressing

Finally it's the weekend
But now I am redundant
It really is a godsend
My choices are abundant
I may not have much money
But at least I have a life
And I don't have to go and play
Bullshit bingo

Yeah bullshit bingo
Oh we all speak the lingo
At cringey cheesy cliché land
There's a language no one understands
Where the god of greed is worshipped
As everybody fills their cup
So let's just keep on talking shite
Until we fuck it up

DEAD TIRED

Dead tired
Dead on my feet
Dead simple
Dead beat
Deadlift
Dead zone
Deadlock
Dead Man's Cove
Dead quiet
Deadly
Dead calm
Dead Sea
Dead centre
Deadpan
Dead proud
Dead man
Deadly nightshade
Dead head
Dead man's handle
Brain dead
Dead good
Dead right
Dead star
Dead of night
Dead leg
Dead heat
Drop dead gorgeous
Dead meat
Dead funny
Deadened
Dead bunny
Dead end

Cruella

SHE'S MY BITCH

She wakens in the silent hours
And rises from her sewer
Her good friends pain and misery
And suffering soon follow
The disciples of unhappiness
That follow in her wake
Feast upon the rotting flesh
Of the victims that she takes

In the darkened alleyways
And through the dim lit streets
She dances such a twisted dance
While good folks are asleep
Celebrates the chaos
And the havoc that she wreaks
And just when things are going well
Into your life she creeps

She's peering through the windows
She's hammering on the door
The flesh is good the blood is warm
She's eaten here before
Lets herself into my house
Although she holds no key
An unwelcome guest has come to dinner
And on the menu's me

You can't run and you can't hide
There's no means of escape
She holds me tight throughout the night
Her breath upon my nape
Overwhelmed by her power
As she grips my thinning wrists
From self-respect to nervous wreck
As my dignity is stripped

She coldly whispers in my ear
You know you can't resist
I have your body at my will
But now I want your spirit
I'll take it and I'll break it
And I'll crush it in my arms
You can tap and you can rock my friend
But you can't resist my charms

Lightning strikes to her delight
And fills my mind with fear
The rain beats down on nowhere town
And I wish I wasn't here
The wind it howls and the thunder growls
And I dream of sweet release
But it's hard to dream of anything
Because she never lets you sleep

She cups my heart within her palm
Then rips it from my chest
She's the whore that's slept with a thousand souls
But never once been kissed
She leaves before the sun's first light
Wrapped in a cloak of mist
But she'll return when darkness falls
Colitis she's my bitch

Cruella

THE LAST RESORT

The Tories had a dream
That their praises would be sung
When they put the nations footing
Upon the bottom run
But the dream became a nightmare
And turned from sad to sadder
When the chancellor of the day
Kicked away the ladder
As your interest payments hit the roof
The economy hit the floor
You gave them all you had to give
But still they wanted more
Your equity was negative
You owed thousands by the score
And you beat your fists against the wall
As the bailiffs smashed the door
There's no one you can turn to
There's no place you can go
You thought you'd bought a piece of paradise
But how were you to know
If you had a little time
You'd soon be on your feet
But the bank they want their money
So they put you on the street
And if cardboard city's full
Down by Waterlooville Station
Check into the last resort
Sheltered accommodation
Where your landlord seems so nice at first
He could be heaven sent
But he'll ask for certain favours
If you can't afford the rent
And his mobile's out of service

Ian D Francis

But he promises to phone ya
Although it's obvious he's got cold feet
Because your kid has got pneumonia
The flat has got no heating
So it's really not surprising
So light another candle
And watch the damp uprising
Well there's pushers in the hallway
Syringes in the yard
There's a hooker in the attic
And her customers are hard
The cockroaches have up and left
The rats have gone as well
They didn't mind the violence
But they couldn't stand the smell
There's a young offender moved next door
So you'd better fix your catches
He's not a pyromaniac
He just likes to play with matches
And when the fire starts
You know you're gonna fry
So put your head between your legs
And kiss your arse goodbye
Then leap out of the window
And look up to the sky
And when you thump against the deck
Pray to God you die
Because your friendly landlord's on his way
To evict you from the flat
There's a heavy at his side
With a baseball bat
He asked for certain favours
That you weren't prepared to do
And when they break down the door
God help you

Cruella

And if there's no room left at all
At Hotel Desperation
Check into the last resort
Sheltered accommodation
Because there's muggers in the alleyway
Who'll leave you gagged and bound
There's a rent boy in the lift
And he's always going down
The cockroaches have up and left
The rats have gone as well
They didn't mind the violence
But they couldn't stand the smell
There's a schizo in the basement
Who's name Bill or Joan or Mike
So you keep your door secure
Because you don't when he'll strike
And when the riots start
You know you're gonna die
But you couldn't give a damn
And here's the reason why
You've never done crack before
But tonight you had a try
Now you're leaping off the balcony
To see if you can fly
So if you can live without the luxuries
Of heat and sanitation
Check into the last resort
Sheltered accommodation

Ian D Francis

DROWNING IN THE SAME DEEP WATER AS YOU

Are you feeling so low?
Are you feeling so blue?
When you look in the mirror
Is that really you

You're looking so tired
You're looking so ill
It's hard to swallow
A bitter little pill

Do you question your worth?
Is that how you're thinking
Do you take in deep breaths?
As you feel yourself sinking

Has your beauty faded
Is it still there inside?
Have you stopped counting
As the years go by

Not even a spark
Where once burned a fire
One day is another
When you have no desire

Are your skies dull and grey?
Where once the sun shone
Do you look back at your life?
And wonder where it has gone

Cruella

But you are not alone
For I am there too
You could say I'm drowning
In the same deep water as you

Ian D Francis

THE SWORD IS MIGHTIER THAN THE PEN

This is the last poem that he ever wrote

And this it the pen that scribed the words
…..of the last poem that he ever wrote

And this is the hand that guided the pen that scribed the words
…..of the last poem that he ever wrote

And this is the fist of the clenched hand that guided the pen that scribed the words
…..of the last poem that he ever wrote

And these are the bruises caused by the fist of the clenched hand that guided the pen that scribed the words
…..of the last poem that he ever wrote

And this is the face of the woman all covered in bruises caused by fist of the clenched hand that guided the pen that scribed the words
…..of the last poem that he ever wrote

And this is the blood on the face of the woman all covered in bruises caused by the fist of the clenched hand that guided the pen that scribed the words
…..of the last poem that he ever wrote

And this is the sword dripping in blood on the face of the woman all covered in bruises caused by the fist of the clenched hand that guided the pen that scribed the words
…..of the last poem that he ever wrote

And this is the stump of the severed hand cut by the sword dripping in blood on the face of the woman all covered in bruises caused by

Cruella

the fist of the clenched hand that guided the pen that scribed the words
…..of the last poem that he ever wrote

And this is the man slumped to his knees waving a stump where the severed hand was cut by the sword all dripping in blood on the face of the woman all covered in bruises caused by the fist of the clenched hand that guided the pen that scribed the words
…..of the last poem that he ever wrote

And this is the last poem that he ever wrote

Ian D Francis

AFTER THE BATTLE

Watch the horses
Running free

Count the corpses
One two three

Dig the graves
And dig them deep

And lay the fallen
There to sleep

Cruella

SQUEAK PIGGY SQUEAK

Squeak piggy squeak
For you know not piggy
Of what you speak
And the havoc that you wreak

Too busy scavenging the trough
And simply not caring
Not caring enough
Or indeed at all
You rise, and you'll fall
When the shit storm calls

The architect of your own doom
The organ plays to an empty room
Shall we dance to the tune
Like I danced to yours
All those uninspiring times

Just smiling and nodding
And biding my time
Just waiting in line
To witness your demise
How the mighty have fallen
You have no allies

Ian D Francis

The bridges aren't burned
They were just never built
Because to build takes courage
It's easier to destroy
You bad little piggy
Little piggy boy

So squeak piggy squeak
For you know not piggy
Of what you speak
And the havoc that you wreak

Cruella

MOTHER WAITS

A mother the age of fifteen
Awakes from her shattered dreams
To find nothing's really changed
And the man beside her in the bed
Well wasn't he the one who said
Happiness is out of your reach
And the baby's cries grow weaker
And she knows she really should feed her
And the baby's cries grow weaker
And she knows she really should feed her
But her habit needs feeding too
Well what's a girl to do
Well what do junkies do
Oh please take me home
Where mother waits
Warm and safe

The streets are wracked with danger
And there's no such thing as a handsome stranger
Just dirty old men in dirty old macks
A few dirty coins for a swift one round the back
Of the church where the congregation pray
Well what can you say
And the baby's cries grow weaker
And she knows she really should feed her
A promise he made by the river
She knew he could never deliver
A new star in the night sky shines
And her baby's cries
Are silent
Oh please take me home
Where mother waits
Warm and safe

Ian D Francis

PRINCE CHARMLESS

The church choir sings
The old bell rings
The best man fiddles
With the wedding rings
A nervous smile
The empty aisles
She wonders what
The future brings
A delicate flower
In the wilderness
Stands all alone
In her wedding dress

Then the preacher asks
Is there a lawful reason?
Why this should not be
The hitching season
With a different deal
In another flavour
On a pure white horse
I'd ride to save her
From a life of lies
With Prince Charmless
But she's all alone
In her wedding dress

Cruella

THE DAY AFTER REDUNDANCY

I have an air of failure
It's with me one more time
The failure is returning
I recognise the signs
I've got that sinking feeling
These failings are all mine
And failure is final
The millionth billionth time
Sometimes you see it coming
But I missed all the clues
I feel a kind of numbness
I've lost the will to lose
What doesn't kill you makes you strong
At least that's what they say
But I am sick of failing
Of failing once again
And again, and again and again and again and again and again

Ian D Francis

LIFE OR DEATH

Life or death
Make a choice
A life of luxury
Or luxury's disappointment
A disappointing end
The end of the world
Or world peace
A piece of the action
Action stations
Station commander
Commander of the seas
A sea of change
Change your mind
Mind over matter
A matter of fact
The facts of life
Life or death
Make a choice

Life or death
Make a choice
Choose death
Death at one's elbow
Or elbow room
Room hire
A hired hand
The hand of God
All God's creatures
Creature comforts
A comfortable life
Life or death
Make a choice

Cruella

BLOOD IS THICKER THAN OIL

Sathanas awaits in the craters
In the trenches the stench is of death
In the land of the godforsaken
Scorched by the dragon's breath

The vultures have gathered in no man's land
A rotting corpse hangs on the wire
A firing squad for the shell-shocked
In this hell hole of blood death and fire

Blood and guts stain the battlefield
Of the dead or those waiting to die
And as the young men march off to battle
The devil is waving goodbye

But our history books tell us the stories
Of heroes swathed in glories
To the victor the spoils of war
Is this what we're fighting for

America (Mr Bush) what have you done
Britain (Mr Blair) you should have stayed home
Because the price of the oil from Iraq
Are the widows dressed all in black

So before you go sticking your flag
In some far off foreign soil
Count up the body bags
Because blood is thicker than oil

Ian D Francis

WHEN DINOSAURS RULED THE EARTH

The dinosaurs called a meeting
To discuss the latest threat
Their numbers were slowly dwindling
Now only a few were left
Triceratops had an agenda
But the details were not common knowledge
The location was a guarded secret
But it took place near the local college
Stegosaurus read out the minutes
The minutes dragged on for hours
Then agenda item one
Resisting a shift in power
Brontosaurus stated
There's order in the pack
Pterodactyl sharpened her beak
And plunged it in his back
Tyrannosaurus roared
Jurassic Park is mine
For I can roar the loudest
And I've ruled since the dawn of time
And I've ruled since the dawn of time

As the dinosaurs continued to argue
Megalosaurus tried to think
He consulted with his dictionary
And looked up the word extinct
Upon discovery of its meaning
He gave out a terrified shriek
The dinosaurs looked at him curiously
But he was too afraid to speak
The Trachodon shouted order
And said I propose a motion
We'll never agree upon anything here

Cruella

If we continue with such commotion
She said I suggest another meeting
One million years from today
And that between now and then
We continue to work the same
So if there's no other business
Then without further adieu
This meeting is now closed
And soon the company too
And soon the company too

Ian D Francis

HIDDEN BONUS TRACK

Cruella

ABOUT THE AUTHOR

To be honest, there's not really that much to know

Other titles by the same author;
A Weapon of Mass Seduction

Scheduled for release in 2019;
The Wednesday Girl

Other literary works currently in progress that may or may not ever get finished;
Sixth Day, and on the Seventh Day Man Invented God
When Dinosaurs Ruled the Earth - A Tale of Toxic Leadership

Printed in Great Britain
by Amazon